I0689864

Eugene Post

The Wig and the Jimmy

Vol. 1

Eugene Post

The Wig and the Jimmy
Vol. 1

ISBN/EAN: 9783337403263

Printed in Europe, USA, Canada, Australia, Japan

Cover: Foto ©Andreas Hilbeck / pixelio.de

More available books at **www.hansebooks.com**

THE WIG AND THE JIMMY:

OR,

A LEAF IN THE

POLITICAL HISTORY OF NEW YORK.

"Alitur vitium vivitque legendo."

Entered according to Act of Congress in the year 1869, by
EUGENE J. POST,
In the Clerk's office of the District Court of the United States for the District of New Jersey.

NEW YORK:
PUBLISHED BY THE AUTHOR.
1869.

PREFACE.

At the instance of the UNION LEAGUE CLUB of New York the House of Representatives, on the 14th day of December, 1868, appointed a Committee of seven to investigate alleged frauds in the Presidential Election of 1868 in the State of New York. Such Committee entered at once upon the discharge of its onerous duties and held sessions in New York City, Peekskill, Kingston, Rondout, Troy, Rochester, Middletown, Port Jervis, Montgomery, Hamptonburg, Newburg and Goshen in the State of New York, and Washington, D. C. The testimony taken by it while very voluminous in extent, covering nearly nine hundred printed pages, was of a directness and importance rarely obtained in similar investigations and necessitated a report of great length and explicitness. Owing to these and other causes it was not until about a week prior to the expiration of the term of the Fortieth Congress that the Committee was able to submit the result of its labors to the House, which at so late a period in the session could take no action upon the bills reported or recommendations made. The large expense attending the printing and binding of the report and testimony led the House Committee on Printing to deem it unwise to publish more than two thousand copies, a number so small as to allow each Member of Congress but four volumes. Unfortunately, the press was unable, owing to the length of the report, to give little more than a hastily prepared telegraphic abstract of the Committee's conclusions. Thus, from causes inherent in the very nature and extent of the work, the circulation and publicity which its importance demanded were estopped, and the legislation which the necessities of the case required was delayed. Knowing that no correct, true or intelligent idea of the facts is prevalent, and believing that only through a general and wide spread knowledge of the illegal and partially successful attempt of the Democracy of New York to thrust minority candidates — both State and National—into places of power and trust, can the American peopl become acquainted with the dangers through which they have passed, or be prepared to protect themselves in the future against the machinations of evil and designing men, the following pages, narrating in a brief and comprehensive form the more important facts sworn to before the Committee, have been prepared.

Without malice, with no motive other than a desire to see perpetuated the institutions of our country, and in the full realization of Bacon's charge that "men's reputations are tender things and ought to be like Christ's coat, without seam," has this pamphlet been written, in good faith, believing the statements contained therein to be true. Confident that the interests of society, good order and puregovernment will beadvanced by its publication, it is respectfully submitted for the earnest consideration of a thoughtful public in every portion of our national domain.

THE AUTHOR.

CHAPTER I.

An incident which transpired during the Spring of 1864 in one of the Southern cities convinced the writer, who was an eye witness, that the fear of exposure and the dread of public opinion were the most wholesome and effective means of punishing and preventing evil.

A woman of some thirty years of age was captured one evening shortly after dark, endeavoring to run the lines of the army. A careful search of her person being made, four large bags were found beneath her under garments, suspended from her waist. The contents were mixed—being letters, shoes, thread, needles and quinine.

A young officer on the staff of the Commanding General of the Department, to whom the captured property was forwarded for examination, succeeded the same night in finding and arresting a young woman of high social standing and personal accomplishments as the author of a most unwomanly letter found among this intercepted mail, containing information sought to be conveyed to the enemy, of certain movements about to be made by the Federal forces. The letter was addressed to a lover in the Rebel army, and written in the closest possible manner upon eight pages of French note paper. The sojourn in the neighborhood of the "cursed Yankees" was deplored and regretted, in that Southern girls had been found quite willing to flirt and coquette with the "vandals," and in instances had so far degraded themselves as to form life partnerships. Miscegenation was discussed with much gusto as purely of Northern origin. Four pages were devoted to a minute and detailed rehearsal of private gossip and scandal respecting her more conservative or politic neighbors, who so far recognized the situation as to act under the belief that a Union soldier *might* be a gentleman. Details, so far as she had been able to gather, respecting an expedition about to move upon the rebel capitol, were added as her mite to aid the cause of secession. The information imparted that a letter, which would not have been taken from the Post Office save for the belief that it came from the South under flag of truce, had been recently received from her aunt in Cincinnati, who wrote that two cousins had both served in the Union army, and one had "died fighting bravely for his country at Chattanooga." And finally, as calculated to specially commend her to the affections of her lover, was added, "and I am glad he is dead, fighting in such a cause;" while a closing prayer was uttered that he whom the Almighty had for some unknown reason seen fit to afflict the South with, in the person of General Butler, "may never die a natural death, or be gathered home to his fathers, but may suffer all the torture possible for mortal man to endure."

The facts being reported to the Commander of the Department, that officer directed the immediate release of the author of the letter and return to her home; and, as a punishment for her offense and a warning to others, ordered that the communication be published in the official papers, signed with her full name and address, and an appendatory statement that all future transgressors of the law requiring messages across the lines to be sent under flag of truce would be similarly dealt with. Mark the result. A spontaneous and universal outburst of popular indignation followed, which but for the firm yet merciful hand of military rule, would, regardless of the sex of the offender, have visited her with condign and summary punishment, while the innocent members of the families of a mother and brother were openly insulted and threatened with personal violence. Indeed, so lasting and deep was the popular feeling that total social ostracism and seclusion became obligatory upon the transgressor, and from that hour until the close of the war no communication of any character was known to clandestinely leave the city, while the flag of truce mail for the South from that locality increased the following week to more than two-thirds its former proportions, and so continued.

So that it is seen that what danger of capture, trial by military commission, long imprisonment and risk of life itself had theretofore been unable to prevent, was at once brought to an end by mere dread of publicity and fear of the scorn and contempt of society.

In the belief that known facts are oftentimes the most powerful weapons of offense or defense ; that rogues and villains fear exposure ; that the arousing of public opinion against any species of crime is the most effective means of thwarting, if not preventing it ; and that quick, decisive, yet unremitting warfare should be waged until desired results are attained, we enter upon the work of detailing the history of the election frauds in New York in 1868, the character of the leaders and more active participants therein, and their connection therewith.

During the month of October, 1868, and within a few hours of the State election in Pennsylvania, when both of the great political parties in that commonwealth were bending all their energies to win success, there left the City of New York in the interests of the Democratic party a large number of gamblers, roughs and professional scoundrels of every description, prominent among whom was a member of the Common Council. These gentry on arriving in Philadelphia at once took an active interest in the struggle, and on the day of election were found voting illegally in the several wards and precincts. Subsequently, many of them were indicted by the Grand Jury of Philadelphia for their offences, but before warrants were issued they had hied to their respective homes in the more hospitable City of New York. Believing " an ounce of prevention worth a pound of cure," the Quaker City authorities did not follow the matter vigorously, preferring to hold over them the indictments as security for future good conduct than to risk their trial by jury during the exciting hours of a Presidential election then close at hand.

The experiment on behalf of the Democracy had been far from unsuccessful, and emboldened and encouraged thereby it was determined to carry it out on a larger scale in November in their own strongholds of political power where Grand Juries, Courts and Judges would not or dared not interfere therewith. The programme as accomplished was as shrewd, comprehensive and bold as wicked, illegal and villainous.

The main features were the employment of repeaters and the wholesale issue of fraudulent certificates of naturalization. The details embodied,

First—A wicked, confessedly untrue and libellous proclamation from the Mayor of the City of New York, the Democratic candidate for Governor.

Second—A secret circular issued from the rooms of the Democratic State Committee requesting telegraphic estimates of the majorities in the several towns and cities in the State, to be sent to Wm. M. Tweed, at Tammany Hall, at the minute of closing the polls.

Third—Instructions from A. Oakey Hall, then District Attorney and Secretary of the Democratic Executive Committee, now Mayor of the City of New York, to all Democratic canvassers in the city, to "prolong the count as far as possible," whereby the leaders, knowing the estimated majorities against them in the "State," had it within their power, by means of fraudulent canvassing, altered returns and ballot-box stuffing—most if not all of which were employed—to override and defeat the popular will; and

Fourth—The swearing in by James O'Brien, Sheriff of the County of New York, himself an ex-inmate of the Penitentiary, of some two thousand special deputies—an unusual and unnecessary proceeding—most of whom, judging from the history, antecedents and behaviour of those known to us, were thieves, and other disreputable characters, whose principal occupation appears to have been to protect, aid and abet fraudulent voting, and annoy, threaten and arrest honest and faithful election officers and peaceable law-abiding citizens.

It is not proposed, however, to here consider these details, but to confine ourselves to the two prominent and distinctive measures previously mentioned.

CHAPTER II.

REPEATING.

This form of fraud is first referred to in the annals of our National politics, in a report of the Judiciary Committee of the United States Senate appointed to investigate the frauds in the Presidential election of 1844, when it was proven to have been practiced, although to a limited extent. Since then it has been comparatively unknown. The followers of St. Tammany, after nearly a quarter of a century, revived it in 1868, when its novelty, nature and *modus operandi* seem to have peculiarly attracted the attention of both rank and file.

A repeater is one, who, without right and against law, makes a business of registering or voting, or both. As in bounty jumping and desertion, occupations quite familiar to most repeaters, the number of times a registry or vote may be repeated in a single day depends largely upon the nerve of the man engaged. And a moment's reflection upon the fact that during the War hundreds of men, with the knowledge that an ignominious death would follow detection, hesitated not to enlist, receive bounty and desert more than a half score of times, must convince the most doubting mind that the same class would from innate depravity, if no other reason was found, engage in a work so full of excitement and adventure as " repeating," especially when practically informed by an honorable Justice of the Supreme Court, as will be hereafter seen, that although arrested in the very commission of the crime neither conviction nor punishment would follow. The proof of repeating is sufficiently abundant to fully justify the report of the Congressional Committee which thoroughly investigated the facts, that if it had devoted its entire time for three months to this matter alone, " it would not have been possible to ascertain or take testimony to prove the *number of persons who voted more than once*" in the City of New York, and that the character of the evidence fully proved the fact that " an organized system was perfected and carried into effect by members of the Democratic party to register many thousands of names, fictitious or assumed, and then to vote on them by hundreds of persons voting from two to forty times each day for the Democratic candidates."

The instances given below, while convincing the reader of the accuracy of these opinions, will illustrate the manner in which the work was carried on and the character of the men and means employed therein.

William H. Greene, a patrolman, attached to the Seventh Precinct Police, was one of the officers on duty at the place of registry of the Sixth District of the Seventh Ward during the first two days of registration. On one of those days he observed a gang of men, several of whom were known to him by name, and all of whom he knew had no residence in the district, register themselves from the houses of Wm. M. Tweed (Grand Sachem of Tammany Hall, State Senator, Deputy Street Commissioner and Supervisor), Patrick H. Keenan Coroner of the City and County of New York), and Edward J. Shandley (Police Justice). Most of them were registered without objection on the part of any one, but some few being challenged promptly took the statutory oaths and compelled the registration of their names. The character of these repeaters may be learned from Greene, who has stated under oath that most of them were "thieves who have several aliases," while " the leader of the gang who registered from Coroner Keenan's house, as Henry J. Lawrence, is an Englishman, known by the name of Charles Wilson, alias 'Nibbs' or 'Nibbsey,' a celebrated pickpocket who has stolen fortunes, but somehow or other always slips through and is never prosecuted." On the opposite page may be seen a copy of the likeness of this favorite of the judicial and political ring as it appears in the Rogues' Gallery at Police Headquarters. An unwillingness to leave his counterpart exhibited itself to such an extent when sitting for his photograph, that two stalwart members of the force were compelled to steady his head and control his facial expression.

Another of this gang, by name Patsey Nolan, alias John Reilly, was a notorious thief, since arrested for stealing a diamond pin. Fortunately we are able to trace these worthy Democrats still further. Late at night on Friday the 30th of October, when but a day of registry remained, Inspector George W. Walling, one of the most earnest and

CHAS. WILSON, ALIAS HENRY J. LAWRENCE, ALIAS "NIBBSEY"
Pickpocket and Repeater.

faithful officers of the Metropolitan force, learned that a gang of repeaters under the leadership of William Varley, alias "Reddy the Blacksmith" (so called from the color of his hair and his former occupation),
well-known as the proprietor of a low drinking saloon on Chatham
Street, the headquarters of one of the worst gangs of thieves and cut
throats known to the police, had been engaged in registering from a
house on Catherine Street, and proposed the following day changing
its rendezvous to No. 29 East Broadway, and resuming operations.
For the purpose of verifying his information. Walling, early on Saturday morning, the 31st, accompanied by six officers in citizens dress, proceeded to the locality named and spent several hours in patiently
watching the suspected house. Shortly before two o'clock, P. M., signs
of activity were manifest and the detectives observed a number of men
leave the house and proceed to the place of registry of the First district
of the Seventh Ward. From there they returned to East Broadway,
and shortly reappearing proceeded to another place of registry in an
adjoining district. Satisfied now of the work these men were engaged
in, Walling allowed them to return to their rendezvous, when he at
once made a descent, drove in and captured a posted watcher before he
could give an alarm, arrested the entire gang—eight in all—and seized
their book. The men were taken at once to Police Headquarters and
incarcerated, and the book turned over to the Superintendent.

An examination and comparison of this book with the original registers for the 1st, 3d, 4th, 6th and 7th districts of the Seventh Ward,
established the startling fact that these eight men had registered one
hundred and sixty-one fictitious or assumed names, assigning as residences fifty-five different houses in East Broadway, Henry, Market,
Monroe and Division Streets, and that they were a part of the same
gang of repeaters observed by Officer Greene on the first or second
day of registration, registering from the houses of Tweed, Keenan
and Shandley. Convinced that "Reddy the Blacksmith," although not
with these repeaters when arrested, was one of their number, Walling
went at once to his saloon. Not finding him in, he searched the place
and seized another book similar in size and appearance to the one previously obtained, containing some sixty additional names with the
number of a house and street opposite each, which names were subsequently ascertained to be mainly registered in the 8th District of the
Sixth and 4th District of the Seventh Wards. The similarity existing
in the assumed names found in the two books thus obtained, and other
strong circumstantial evidence renders it quite certain that the
latter book was also the property of the arrested eight, thus making *two
hundred and twenty* fraudulent and illegal registrations accomplished
by this gang.

Of the character of these repeaters, Walling confirmed Officer Greene,
in that one of them he "knew very well by reputation as a pickpocket,"
while Detective Irving stated that another was a deputy of Sheriff
O'Brien, from whom was taken at headquarters "his shield, and also
some orders of arrest found on his person."

And now reader, mark well how faithfully Tammany protects its
supporters and adherents at the expense of law, justice and good order.
Between six and seven o'clock in the evening of the day of arrest, Wm.
F. Howe, well-known as a criminal lawyer and Democrat, appeared at

Headquarters and served upon Detective Irving, the officer in charge, a writ of *habeas corpus* directing the bodies of the eight to be brought " before the Honorable George G. Barnard, Justice of our Supreme Court, at the office of said Justice Barnard, No. 23 West Twenty-first Street, in the City of New York, this 31st day of October, 1868, at 7 o'clock in the evening."

In compliance with the requirements of the writ, no time being allowed for a return thereto *and none being made*, the men were forthwith taken by Detectives Irving and Coyle to Judge Barnard's residence. Arriving there at about 9 o'clock, Coyle remained on the sidewalk with the prisoners, while Irving went into the house where he found Mr. Howe, who took from him the writ, endorsed thereon "The prisoners being charged with no offence *on the annexed return*, I order them discharged, October 31st, 1868," and handed it to a servant girl who took it up stairs to Judge Barnard's room, and soon came down with the Judge's signature attached to it, obtained as she stated from the Judge, *who had gone to bed.* Thereupon the prisoners were discharged.

It is worthy of note that no notice of the issue or hearing of the writ was served upon the District Attorney as the representative of the people, which notice so distinguished a Democrat as Judge McCunn has testified he thought a Judge " bound by law to give to the District Attorney of his county; the statute requires it," and which the then District Attorney, A. Oakey Hall, has sworn, " should be *preliminary* to the hearing, and it is a *misdemeanor* for a judge to hear a writ without notice to the party interested."

The arrest of these repeaters was serviceable in that it prevented them from continuing operations during the afternoon and evening, while the discharge was instructive in affording definite information as to the precise locality of " the office of said Justice Barnard, No. 23 West Twenty-first Street," where as we are informed in " The Ermine in the Ring," the judicial robes of this eminent and high minded magistrate are at times "endued for the occasion when at his utmost altitudes." The prisoners in the custody of an officer were *on the sidewalk,* their counsel and the officer served with the writ, were *in the hallway,* the writ itself with no return thereon was *in the hands of a servant girl,* and the Chief " Justice of our Supreme Court" was transacting chamber business *in his bed.*

The result was, *First* : Discharge of the prisoners and some *sixty* fraudulent and illegal votes polled on the names by them registered. *Second* : A feeling of security on the part of thousands of employed repeaters whereby, to obtain for themselves the promised pecuniary or other reward, their exertions were redoubled to illegally swell the Democratic majority in the City.

But lest it be charged that an extreme case has been instanced, let us examine another.

During the sittings of the Congressional Committee in New York, in January last, an Attorney of the Supreme Court, who at the time of election was an Inspector in the 5th District of the 18th Ward, testified before it, that very late in the evenings of the days for registration, there came to the Board of which he was a member, in groups of four

WILLIAM VARLEY, ALIAS "REDDY THE BLACKSMITH."

Pickpocket, Thief and Democratic "Regulator" (See Appendix.)

or five, as applicants for registration, a large number of young men of from 21 to 25 years of age. These groups were usually led by one Florence Scannell, an ex-member of the Common Council, and a somewhat notorious character. Each of these men being challenged, sworn and examined, stated that he resided at the Compton House, a combination of rum hole, restaurant and cheap lodging house on the corner of Third Avenue and Twenty-fourth Street, of which Fagin and Scannell, both of whom were Deputy Sheriffs, and the latter a brother of Florence, were the proprietors. Further questioning elicited from several the information that "they slept there (the Compton House) two or three nights out of the week, and the rest of the time slept with their mistresses." Deeming this matter worthy of investigation, Florence Scannell was brought before the Committee and sworn.

Being examined, he admitted having employed some thirty men to register names, but stated that he could not tell where they registered for the reason that they had registered *from* 150 *to* 200 *names*, and from "*almost every house in the district.*" That on the day of election he had engaged some twenty men who had voted on about *one hundred* of those registered names. Believing he was stating only so much of his operations as he chose and concealing the rest, the original registry book of his district was obtained, when the Compton House *alone* was found to have 152 *names registered therefrom*, while the poll book showed that *ninety-four* votes had been cast from that house, *twenty-seven of which were never registered.*

The registry book being exhibited to Scannell, and also to one Mc-Glade, bar tender of the Compton House, the two swore that they only knew thirty-nine of the one hundred and seventy-nine names registered and voted therefrom, and some of this small number were not residents of the house.

Of the thirty-nine known to them, but twenty-seven voted, and seven of these illegally—six not being registered. So that under Democratic manipulation there were registered from this single house *one hundred and fourteen fraudulent names* and *seventy-four fraudulent and illegal votes polled.*

How an endeavor to so alter the present registry law as to render it easy in the future to discover, thwart and almost wholly prevent any similar attempt was opposed by the Democratic members of the last Legislature, and after the passage of the bill by the Republicans, was strangled by the veto of a Democratic Governor who held his seat solely by means of these and similar fraudulent votes will be seen hereafter.

Yet still another instance, for the field is large and profitable.

A young man, addicted for years to the dangerous yet fascinating and fashionable sin of gambling, but otherwise of good character, was engaged during the latter part of October by Peter Norton, brother of the notorious Michael Norton, State Senator from the Fifth Senatorial District and Alderman from the Eighth Ward, to join a gang of repeaters operating in the Fourteenth, Eighth and Sixth Wards.

The instructions given were " to register as often as possible on the two last registry days." Having served his country well and faithfully for some eight years in the marine corps and regular army, and being " inclined to the side of order and good government," our young friend failed reporting to Norton during the day of the 30th of October. In the evening he repaired to the liquor store of Peter Mitchell, present Democratic Member of Assembly, then a candidate, on the corner of Bleecker and Greene Streets, where he found congregated some forty repeaters. Excusing himself for absence during the day, he was ordered to report the next morning at 7 o'clock, whereupon he left and related the facts to the Superintendent of Police and several prominent citizens. The result was the receipt from them of instructions to join the repeaters, and in the character of a detective learn all possible of their operations. Accordingly on the morning of the 31st he reported at Mitchell's, but found only one of the gang, David Sommers by name, present, who claimed to be Peter Norton's lieutenant. Taking a drink with Sommers who stated that Peter had been up all night with the boys, and was then sleeping, the two visited Peter Burns at his saloon, No. 69 East Houston Street, who gave them each slips of paper bearing a name and residence written thereon. Under these names they registered in the Second District of the Fourteenth Ward, Sommers swearing in his registry. Shortly after three others of the gang joined them, and the five registered in the Second and Third Districts of the Eighth Ward. At the latter place the party was still further augmented in number and visited the First District of the Eighth Ward where they registered as from 84 Greene Street, the residence of Peter Mitchell. Sommers and our detective then called at Peter Norton's, and arousing him, the three joined the others at Mitchell's saloon where they found Senator Norton and Mitchell. Some 25 or 30 slips with names and residences on which to register were then furnished by the two Nortons and Mitchell, and the information imparted that the occupants of the houses from which they were to register understood the matter, and would answer satisfactorily any inquiries which might be made by the police or others. The strength of the gang constantly increasing, they were then divided into parties numbering from four to twelve each, and dismissed in different directions. Attached to a party of five was our detective, and after registering in Varick Street they returned to Mitchell's where Peter Norton transferred the detective to a party of twelve, bound for the Sixth Ward. Walking rapidly, this crowd soon arrived at No. 44 Bowery, known as "Cuddy's Hotel," where they found Edward Cuddy, present member of the Board of Aldermen from the Sixth Ward. This worthy at once produced a book containing some hundreds of names and residences, and from behind his bar handed, or passed over his shoulder to each man a small card or slip bearing a name and residence taken from his book. Thus supplied, the party left and registered in the Ninth District of the Sixth Ward as from 60 and 70 Mott Street and 62 Bayard Street, some being compelled to swear in their registry. This completed the day's work, and our detective returned to Mitchell's where he was directed by Peter Norton to call upon him for his reward, and not fail to be on hand on the day of election. It may be added, for statements made by confederates to each other are good and admissible evidence, that it was stated to our detective that they had done better than is here set forth on the previous day, and since election several of them have boasted of registering and voting from twenty to twenty-five times each. All the facts just stated were fully established under oath by this amateur detective who produced before the

Congressional Committee as coroborative evidence, original notes secretly made by him at the time of the occurrences and some of the identical slips furnished him. An examination of the original registers for the districts mentioned, not only showed every name given by him to be registered as he stated, thus completely confirming him, but also evidenced the fact that from every house of which this crowd of repeaters represented themselves residents, there was a large registration, while from inquiries at the several places and other proof it was established that such registration was in excess of the actual number of legal voters resident, from 6 to 27 names in the different houses.

These are but samples of hundreds of instances which might be given. We could readily detail how men repeatedly registered in the same Election District with no other or further attempt at disguise than the changing of their hats, caps and coats on the public street, and almost within sight of the registrars: how in some districts an examination of the registry was made and the names of the persons legally registered who had not voted were copied and passed to outside parties, whereupon repeaters assuming such names voted thereon; and how inspectors, challengers and others who endeavored to prevent these and similar scenes were threatened, assaulted and arrested; but neither the fact that repeating was practiced by the Democratic party on a most gigantic scale, nor the intricate, subtle or varied means employed to accomplish its illegal purposes would be more clearly comprehended. The cases narrated must suffice.

Yet, we cannot refrain from anticipating the question each reader will undoubtedly ask. Was there no repeating in the interests of the Republican party in the City of New York? The answer is, that while there were doubtless individual instances, there was no attempt made in that direction, either organized and general or by any of its leaders or candidates so far as is known. And while the Congressional Committee, two of whom were Democrats—and one, the Hon. M. C. Kerr, of Indiana, the candidate of his party for the Speakership of the House of Representatives—was in being from the 14th of December, 1868, to the 4th of March, 1869, and held sessions in New York for one third of that time, it is a remarkable and honorable fact in the language of the Committee's supplemental report " *that there is no evidence of any kind that any republican was engaged in false registering in the interest of the republican party, and without false registering there could be no repeating.*"

CHAPTER III.

THE ISSUE AND USE OF FRAUDULENT CERTIFICATES OF NATURALIZATION.

In treating of this subject, but two matters seem essentially worthy of consideration, viz: the extent of the issue, and the men and means employed in the work. And as Courts in a number of the river and central counties of the State were parties to this form of fraud to quite as great an extent comparatively as some of those in the City of New York, we propose in our examination to divide the subject, discussing first

The Naturalization Frauds in New York City.

That we may judge of the number of fraudulent certificates issued in the City of New York, let us glance for a moment at the statistics of former years and the preparations made for naturalization in 1868. Judge Daly of the Court of Common Pleas, in his exhaustive and able article upon naturalization in Vol. xii of the New American Cyclopædia, states that in ten years from 1850 to 1859 inclusive, there were naturalized in the City of New York over 60,000 aliens.

For the eight years from 1860 to 1867, inclusive, the total number was 70,604. The total number of Naturalizations in New York City for each year from 1856 to 1867, inclusive—a period of twelve years, was :—

Year.	No.	Year.	No.
1856, Presidential	16,493	1862	2,414
1857	8,991	1863	2,633
1858	6,769	1864, Presidential	12,171
1859	7,636	1865	7,423
1860, Presidential	13,556	1866	13,023
1861	3,903	1867	15,476

a total average of 9,207 per annum. This was the work of two Courts, viz: the Superior and Court of Common Pleas. The Supreme Court in the First Judicial District had never to this time in the history of the State naturalized a person. Notwithstanding the fact that the yearly average of naturalizations had been but about 9,000 ; that the greatest number naturalized in a single year never reached 16,500 ; that three years had elapsed since the close of the war in which 35,927 aliens had been made citizens, a yearly average of 11,975, or an excess of 3,000 per year above the annual average for twelve years ; that the addition of such excess to the diminished numbers naturalized in 1862, 1863 and 1864 would preserve the ratio, and account for those who from fear of being drafted had refrained from applying during those years of the war ; that the rebellion had reduced the alien population of New York City, many of whom enlisted, were killed, died from disease, or after the war found homes elsewhere ; and, finally, that the yearly average of emigration from and including 1847 to 1860—a period of thirteen years—had been 197,435, while for the four years from 1860 to 1863 inclusive—and none who arrived subsequently could be legally naturalized in 1868—the yearly average of alien arrivals had been but 100,962, or an annual loss of one-half, yet orders were early in September passed along the Democratic line to prepare on a gigantic scale for the naturalization of aliens during the coming month. The Supreme Court also determined for the first time to engage in the work of making citizens. In accordance with this known determination, there were printed for the use of the Courts on the days below named the following number of blanks :

SUPERIOR COURT.			SUPREME COURT.		
Date.	No, applications.	No. certificates.	Date.	No. applications.	No. certificates.
Oct. 2	......	10,000	Sept. 16	10,000	9,000
" 3	10,000	......	" 19	10,000	......
" 8	......	10,000	Oct. 6	25,000	5,000
" 15	......	10,000	" 12	5,000	5,000
" 16	20,000	......	" 13	10,000	......
			" 15	......	10,000
			" 16	5,000	......
			" 19	5,000	......
			" 20	......	10,000
			" 22	5,000	......

or a total of 30,000 applications and 30,000 certificates for the Superior Court, and 75,000 applications and 39,000 certificates for the amateur Court (Supreme).

The Court of Common Pleas, which save for a year or two previous had done the larger share of the work of naturalization, did but little in 1868, its total number for the year being 3,145, of which 1,615 were in October. Justice requires the further statement that there was no evidence whatever of any fraud in this Court, although all its Judges were elected as Democrats, while proof was abundant that the duty entrusted to it of making citizens of the United States was discharged throughout with marked propriety and dignity.

In the Supreme and Superior Courts only were frauds proven. To what extent we will now consider. The following table was sworn to as being the daily number of applications for naturalization on file in the Supreme Court Clerk's office for 1868.

1868—October 6	6	1868—October 16	721
" October 7	8	" October 17	633
" October 8	379	" October 19	955
" October 9	668	" October 20	944
" October 10	717	" October 21	773
" October 12	723	" October 22	675
" October 13	901	" October 23	587
" October 14	523		
" October 15	857	Total	10,070

But these applications do *not* show the number of naturalizations granted by this Court, although they should so do. They simply show that for 10,070 certificates issued there are a corresponding number of papers purporting to be applications, on file. Let us examine a moment in detail. The 10,070 certificates admittedly issued (there are known to be 10,093 applications, pretended or otherwise, on file), is but 1,070 in excess of the number of blank certificates printed for use by this Court on the 16th of September—three weeks before it naturalized a man—and is 4,000 *less* than the number on hand on the 6th day of October when it begun operations, although (25,000) *twenty-five thousand* additional were subsequently printed by order of the Clerk, and 10,000 of these within forty-eight hours of the time when the Court ceased to naturalize.

As Charles E. Loew, Clerk of the County and ex-officio Clerk of the Supreme Court, testified that these blanks were " never given out," and that certificates of naturalization were " to be given out *only by the Clerk on the order of the Court*," the inquiry as to whether the remaining 28,930 blank certificates shown to be printed were in the custody of the Clerk of the Court to whom they were delivered was deemed mportant and pertinent.

An actual count of the number on hand was therefore required, when the Assistant Deputy Clerk who made the count certified that 1,862 only remained, leaving the large number of 27,068 blanks missing and unaccounted for in any way.

We find, then, an admitted issue by this Court of 10,070 certificates of naturalization in sixteen days, or 10,054 in fourteen days—work not really beginning until October 8th—a daily average of 718. Beyond this is a clearly proven, but on the part of the Court, a concealed, issue of what extent it is impossible to precisely state. Evidence abounds to sustain the position taken by the Congressional Committee that 27,068, the whole number of missing blanks, is the correct amount.

In the Superior Court a singular state of affairs was found to exist. Being required to furnish the committee with the number of naturalizations in that Court in the year 1868, and the daily issue for the month of October, Owen E. Westlake, a clerk, on the 28th of December, swore to the following statement :

1868—January	84	1868—October 9th	1,760
" February	100	" October 10th	1,653
" March	105	" October 12th	1,856
" April	140	" October 13th	1,868
" May	108	" October 14th	2,109
" June	102	" October 15th	1,429
" July	140	" October 16th	1,112
" August	195	" October 17th	840
" September	632	" October 19th	1,026
" October 1st	580	" October 20th	1,004
" October 2d	745	" October 21st	861
" October 3d	840	" October 22d	911
" October 5th	1,425	" October 23d	1,024
" October 6th	1,721	" November	41
" October 7th	1,630	" December	24
" October 8th	1,842		

a total of 27,897 for the year, or 26,236 in twenty days in the month of October, a daily average of 1,311. On the 2d of January, 1869, Joseph Meeks, the Deputy Clerk, swore " that the figures of Westlake were derived from an actual count ;" and on the 14th of the same month officially certified the total for the year 1868 to be as above stated, which certificate was presented the Committee, under oath, by Adam Gillespie, assistant naturalization clerk. If evidence is worth anything, surely this should be sufficient to establish the facts testified to. The Committee having meanwhile appointed a clerk—an attorney of the Supreme Court—to count and examine the applications on file in the Clerk's office for the month of October, was not a little surprised to learn from him, under oath, on the 25th of January, 1869, that but about 18,000 papers had been produced for his inspection, and he was informed that these were all there were. Here was a discrepancy of *eight thousand* for a single month, and the loss apparently made since the number was so positively sworn to from "an actual count." Fearing the result of this exposure, Adam Gillespie, aforementioned, and others, were hastened to Washington to explain away this startling exhibit. Quite naturally their statements then made, that the first exhibit submitted and so positively testified to was a mere estimate and not the "actual count" required and sworn to be, were far from satisfactory, as testimony obtained from other sources concerning the manner in which most of the naturalizations in this Court were made, strongly corroborated the accuracy of the original figures.

As then stated the daily naturalizations for the month of October were—

1868—October	1	426	1868—October 13	1,384
" October	2	723	" October 14	1,569
" October	3	785	" October 15	934
" October	5	1,363	" October 16	581
" October	6	1,272	" October 17	418
" October	7	1,415	" October 19	709
" October	8	1,133	" October 20	517
" October	9	877	" October 21	428
" October	10	804	" October 22	459
" October	12	2,017	" October 23	618

a total of 18,432, a daily average of 921, or 7,794 less than previously sworn to, while the Committee's Clerk between the time of these two "counts" by the Court officers could find but 17,915 applications, or 8,311 less than appeared by the first exhibit of the Court Clerks, and 517 less than was shown by the second. But supposing true this last "count" of the Court officials, the *admitted* naturalizations in the several Courts in New York city alone for the year 1868 were—

Common Pleas	3,145	In October alone	1,645
Superior Court	20,103	" "	18,432
Supreme "	10,070	" "	10,070

or a total of 33,318, nearly four times the average of former years, and more than twice as many as ever before, while two courts, in an average of eighteen days sittings each, in addition to discharging their ordinary duties, granted 28,502 certificates, or more than eighty-two per cent. of the whole yearly number. Adding the 27,068 missing blanks as the concealed issue of the Supreme Court, we have a total naturalization for 1868 in New York city of 60,386, which the evidence taken, and much not obtained but readily to be had, shows to be the more accurate and probable amount. And even this, it should be remembered, is without taking into account the 8,311 additional certificates sworn and certified to by three officers of the Superior Court as granted by that Court in October.

Fortunately there is no question as to who were the leaders in this bold and illegal work, for pre-eminently at its head and front must necessarily be the Judges who took part therein. In the Supreme Court no member of the bench but George G. Barnard naturalized a single individual. His position is consequently easily determined. In the Superior Court five Judges at times naturalized, viz.: John H. McCunn, Samuel B. Garvin, Samuel Jones, John M. Barbour and Anthony L. Robertson, now deceased. All the evidence agrees that far the greater portion of the work was done by Judge McCunn, while the gentleman who examined nearly 18,000 of the applications on file in that Court testified, " I should think about eight-ninths," *or more than* (15,000) *fifteen thousand,* " bore his initials." We cheerfully add, that of all the Superior Court Judges he alone is impeached by the testimony taken. These two then, George G. Barnard of the Supreme and John H. McCunn of the Superior Court, are originally the guilty parties. The story is credited and credible, though from its nature difficult to substantiate, that the exertions of both in this matter were demanded by Tammany as the price of renomination to their respective positions. Certain it is that Judge Barnard was at the time a candidate of his party for re-election, while it is well understood that Judge McCunn, nominated to his present seat on the bench by Mozart Hall, is pledged a renomination this fall by Tammany.

The Supreme Court was for naturalization purposes open solely at night, generally from 7 to 10 o'clock, but occasionally somewhat later. The Superior Court, save upon two or three occasions, was open for this work only during the day, while as a rule Judge McCunn naturalized but in the afternoon. In less than four hours in the Supreme Court and six in the Superior most of this illegal work was done, certificates of naturalization being admittedly granted at a daily average of 718 in the former and 921 in the latter, while as many as 955 were confessedly issued upon one occasion in the Supreme in about four hours, and 2,017 in the Superior in a portion of one day and evening, mainly by Judge McCunn. How strangely in view of these facts does it sound to read from a report made to the House of Representatives in 1844, of the circumstances attending the impeachment and removal of Benjamin C. Elliot, Judge of the City Court of Lafayette, by the Senate of Louisiana sitting as a high Court of impeachment, that " it further appeared that *nearly four hundred* of these certificates (of naturalization) were issued in one day. It seems to your committee impossible that this could have been legally done." If the granting of " nearly four hundred" certificates of naturalization in 1844 brought impeachment and removal upon the offending Judge, it is an easy matter to determine the least punishment demanded for those who in 1868, in a few hours, admittedly granted twice and thrice—aye, nearly four times that number. As time is an important element in determining the character of this work, it should not be lightly passed over. We have said that in the Court of Common Pleas naturalization was honestly conducted. Let us now ascertain the time required to make a citizen and the manner of procedure in that Court, that the contrast between it and the Supreme and Superior may be more apparent. Judge John R. Brady, who for thirteen years has served honorably and faithfully upon the Common Pleas' bench, has testified, " the process has been to have parties appear before the Judge in open Court," and the time required to naturalize a man " depends very much upon the intelligence of the witness. Sometimes it has been done in from three to five minutes ; sometimes it has taken more ; sometimes I have held cases for reflection for half an hour, or an hour, or an hour and a half." Mr. Jarvis, Clerk of this Court, testifying on this subject, said, " *The action of the Court alone would take probably about five minutes.* There were many cases where I knew the Court to be twenty minutes

JAMES MYERS, ALIAS MULLEN.

Till Tapper and Special Deputy Sheriff. (See Appendix.)

in the examination of a witness, and then to reject the applicant." In response to the direct question as to why more naturalizations were granted in the other Courts and less in his in 1868, the same witness replied, " I cannot state any reason ; I may have an impression. I don't think we naturalized them *rapidly enough.*" At the rate stated from twelve to fifteen certificates were granted per hour in the Common Pleas. Who can doubt the correctness of Mr. Jarvis' impression on reflecting that in the Supreme Court admittance was not only refused citizens, attorneys and reporters, but that when present they were at times forcibly ejected; that in the same Court the admitted naturalizations must at times have been granted at an average *of more than three per minute ;* and that Judge McCunn, of the Superior Court, has himself testified he could naturalize *two persons a minute ;* while in practice he must have done even better than that? The Congressional Committee, a majority of whom were lawyers, and some of whom had served upon the bench, thought as a rule " a Judge could not actually and properly naturalize over twelve in an hour"—the average in the Court of Common Pleas. He who taking into consideration these facts does not clearly comprehend why for the first time the Supreme Court was compelled to take part in naturalization; who does not fully understand the extensive preparations early made by the Supreme and Superior Courts for this work ; and finally, who does not in the subsequent illegal and fraudulent practices of these Courts perceive the strongest evidences of a preconceived plan and conspiracy on the part of the Democracy to issue, circulate and employ for purposes of illegal registration and voting thousands of fraudulent certificates of naturalization, is either a knave or a fool. Such as he would not be convinced were " one to rise from the dead." Yet another fact, and one which conclusively establishes the fraudulent nature of a large number of the certificates admittedly granted, is the great proportion of " minor applications." By law if an alien arrives in this country before the age of eighteen he is entitled, if a resident for five years, to be naturalized upon reaching twenty-one, without having two years prior to application declared his " intentions." Of the 10,070 certificates admittedly issued by the Supreme Court, all but 382, or *more than ninety-six per cent.* were issued upon these " minor applications," while of the 18,000 papers examined in the Superior Court 14,000, or *eighty per cent.*, were of the same character. In the Court of Common Pleas about fifty per cent. only of those naturalized were " minors." The efficient aid which the use of these " minor applications" would render in dispensing with the production of a certificate of previously declared intentions was never lost sight of by the conspirators, while the astounding number of *baby* applicants seems in no wise to have disturbed the equanimity of our immaculate, disinterested and honest Judges—McCunn and Barnard.

But the essential aid rendered by these Judges need not be further detailed. It was mainly comprised in one or more of the following criminal derelictions of duty :

I. Hasty and incomplete examination of applicants and witnesses.

II. Total neglect at times to examine the one class or the other.

III. Through negligence, imposition which might easily have been guarded against, or direct complicity, the issue of certificates in the names of persons who never appeared in Court, applied therefor, produced a witness or took an oath.

IV. Similar issue of certificates to applicants, persons of assumed or fictitious names and others, upon the oath of residence and moral character of persons of assumed and fictitious names, or of known criminals and persons of immoral character.

V. Similar issue of certificates based upon "minor applications" when the persons to whom such certificates issued were known or could readily have been ascertained to be unentitled thereto on such applications.

VI. Total neglect or refusal to commit known disreputable persons and others whose business it was for a pecuniary or other consideration to act as witnesses and who in such capacity repeatedly appeared before them.

VII. The conducting of naturalization proceedings in a secret manner, by causing citizens and others to be denied admission to the Court-room, or ejected therefrom when observed.

As auxiliaries in the plot of procuring and furnishing fraudulent certificates were numerous offices under the control of Tammany Hall, or its Committees, and the several Democratic Ward organizations. Also an improvised office in the basement of the City Hall. In most if not in all these places applications were given out and filled up, professional witnesses employed or permitted, and illegal and fraudulent certificates procured from the Courts and distributed, given away or sold. Some of the Democratic candidates and many then office holders, either secretly or openly countenanced and aided these or similar establishments or engaged in outside operations of a like character on their own responsibility. Without attempting to detail the many methods adopted to secure naturalization certificates on the part of speculators, politicians, thieves and repeaters, we shall instance a case or two illustrative of hundreds which might be recited, and in the appendix name the more prominent characters with a statement of their efforts.

A young man, whom for obvious reasons we shall designate as Henry, formerly an attache of the city press, being out of employment during the month of September and observing signs of activity in the neighborhood of the City Hall, determined to engage for himself in the work of procuring naturalization certificates. Having a large acquaintance in the 20th Ward, he made arrangements that the names of persons for whom certificates were desired should be left at a liquor store in 32d Street. Establishing himself at a lager beer saloon in Chatham Street, in close proximity to the Courts, with a stock in trade consisting of an ink bottle, a few pens and a number of blank applications obtained from the offices of the County Clerk and Democratic Committee, this was briefly his mode of doing business.

Receiving each night at his up town headquarters such names as had been left for him during the day, he would on the following morning fill up his blank applications, sign them as witness with his own or a fictitious or assumed name, or procure others to so sign, and when necessary, would in a similar manner sign both as applicant and witness.

During the day or evening he would present these papers to the Courts, sometimes with and sometimes without the company of the applicant. In this manner appearing on occasions as witness, at other times as applicant, and when necessary, as both applicant and witness, Henry has testified he procured *more than six hundred certificates.* These he furnished to different parties, receiving for his services from one to five dollars from each.

It may be added that Henry has further testified to seeing "as many as one hundred" men "called up by Judge Barnard," and sworn in a batch, while other witnesses swore before the Congressional Committee to the same effect, one stating that he saw oaths administered by Judge Barnard to batches of men numbering "from one hundred to about two hundred, and I remember one occasion when I counted over one hundred and eighty in a batch. There would be four or five batches varying from one hundred and ten to two hundred in number, averaging about one hundred and forty or one hundred and fifty, *got through by Judge Barnard in each hour.*"

A man somewhat actively connected with the Democratic party and for years an office holder under Democratic Judges, through a simple desire to do his best to swell the Democratic vote, procured the assistance of two young friends and together the trio prepared and filled up mainly with fictitious or assumed names, some seventy-five applications. These were handed to John B. McKean, Clerk in Judge Barnard's Court, on two occasions and certificates in the names of such parties received on the following days, no person having appeared in Court therefor, or been sworn either as applicant or witness. Most of these papers were subsequently furnished repeaters and others to aid them in registering and voting. The writer sometime since had placed in his hands several of these particular certificates, together with a number of others issued by the Supreme and Superior Courts in the various modes related herein. In instances he has the affidavits of those whose names they bear, detailing the facts relative to their obtaining possession thereof.

A single other fact and we pass to the consideration of affairs in the State. It was sworn to before the Congressional Committee, that contracts were made by two brothers, whose sole business was appearing as professional witnesses, for the delivery of certificates in Kings and Orange Counties, N. Y., and the States of Connecticut and New Jersey, for fifty cents each. Some of these certificates were obtained by employing eight or ten men who under assumed names repeatedly appeared in court and swore themselves through. Others were received direct from the hands of the court clerk, no one appearing either as applicant or witness. Under these circumstances it behooves all in the Counties and States named (and elsewhere, for the writer believes many were sent to Pennsylvania), who would protect the purity of the ballot box, to closely scan in the future all certificates presented and purporting to have been issued by these Courts in 1868. No one should be allowed to register or vote thereon without at least being challenged, sworn and thoroughly examined.

Naturalization Frauds in the State outside of New York City.

The Committee, while not having time to make an extended tour through the State, visited every county where they had information naturalization frauds had been perpetrated. These embraced West-chester, Orange, Dutchess, Rensselaer, Livingston and Monroe. In all of these gross frauds were proven but generally of a character different from those committed in New York City. In almost every case the certificates issued in these counties, amounting in the aggregate to about six thousand are totally null and void, having been issued without authority or warrant of law in any respect. As a rule no court was held, and no Judge was present. The pretended natralizations were made by County Clerks, their assistants, deputies, and in instances, acting assistants. Not a single certificate so granted is worth the paper it is written upon, and no person should be allowed to register or vote thereon. In Westchester, Orange and Dutchess, a large number of certificates were found, purporting to have been obtained from the Supreme and Superior Courts of New York City. In the main these were sent to some prominent democrat who delivered them to the parties whose names they bore or placed them where they could be readily obtained by such persons. Very few of those who thus received certificates applied therefor, appeared in court or were sworn.

The great length of this chapter precludes any further or more elaborate statement, while the points given, if carefully noted, may prove of service in future elections. A single copy of the evidence taken by the Committee, can at least, be obtained by some wide-awake and energetic citizen, from his member of Congress, the details and extent of the frauds learned therefrom, and a plan devised to prevent the injurious use of these certificates.

But our history would be incomplete were we to omit to state the stricking fact that in every county where frauds in naturalization were found to have prevailed, the Judges and County Clerks or those who granted the certificates were Democrats. Not a single illegal or fraudulent certificate was proven to have been issued in a county where the Judges and Clerks were Republicans or by an officer of that political faith. The writer has no comments to make.

The facts are stated, the record is made and the truth alone has been written. The reader must draw his own conclusions, and in the future when called upon to exercise the right of suffrage, let him with the light before him act conscientiously upon his own convictions of right, and justice, and his duty to himself and his country.

CHAPTER IV.

CONSIDERATIONS FOR THE FUTURE AND REMEDIES PROPOSED.

No candid reader of the foregoing chapters can fail to comprehend that unless measures of the most positive character be taken to prevent in the future a repetition of scenes so disgraceful, illegal and criminal, as are there recited, the days of a Republican form of government in our country are already numbered. Based as our government is upon the fundamental idea of popular suffrage and the rule of majorities, if a few men, or a party, with the intent to defeat and subvert the will of the people and aggrandize office and power to themselves, can secretly concoct, boldly plan, and successfully execute on the grandest scale the most dangerous and criminal schemes of fraud; can escape all punishment for their offences, and whenever, and as often as the occasion shall in their opinion seem to demand it, can perpetrate anew their nefarious operations with the aid derivable from the fraudulent instruments previously obtained, then, indeed, are American institutions a failure, and revolution, anarchy and ruin sure to follow.

We have no desire to be considered an alarmist. But no sane man, in view of what has been shown to have transpired in New York, and with the knowledge that courts in California and Pennsylvania also engaged in issuing fraudulent certificates of naturalization to no inconsiderable extent, can doubt that the effort was seriously made by or on behalf of the Democratic party to carry the last Presidential election by fraud.

And if the certificates so issued cannot, or are not to be treated as other than legal and valid, what is to prevent in the future one or more courts in each State, or county if deemed necessary, engaging in similar attempts? Or again, if two courts in New York can, in an average period of less than three weeks, issue some 60,000 certificates of citizenship upon which votes may be cast, what is to hinder those courts in a period of a few short months from granting such a number of naturalizations as would make the attempt to elect national officers of a political faith other than Democratic as futile and useless as it now is in the metropolis of the nation to endeavor to place a Republican in the Mayor's chair?

Let none be deceived by the thought that such certificates could not be used on the day of election. From 1845 to 1865 the average per centum of votes cast in the State of New York, as compared with the actual number of voters, was less than 77 per cent. The average in Presidential years, from 1848 to 1864 inclusive, was 87.19 per cent. In 1868 this average in the State, owing to frauds, was *ninety-two* (92) *per cent.*, while in the city of New York the per centage was *one hundred and eight* (108). In other words, the number of votes cast in the city of New York at the Presidential election of 1868 was, as compared with the actual number of voters therein, more than twenty per cent. in excess of the average in the State at any previous Presidential election, sixteen per cent. more than the average in the State at the same election—although, as a rule, more votes proportionately are polled in the country than in the city— and *eight per cent. more than the whole number of voters in the city*, supposing every such person to have voted.*

The frauds we have shown lost the Republican party New York and New Jersey with their forty electoral votes, nearly one seventh of the whole number of the electoral college and one-half of the official strength of the Democracy in that body. What then is to be done? It is idle to talk of punishing repeaters and others when Judges of our highest courts are themselves the most wilful and flagrant violators of the law. Not a man has been placed on trial in New York city by the State officials for a violation of the election laws at the election of 1868,

* Calculations based upon census of 1865.

though hundreds of such criminals are well known to the authorities. But this is the rule, thoroughly established and well understood, with hardly an exception known. The probabilities of conviction or punishment we are wholly relieved from considering. Indeed, a Grand Jury mainly composed of prominent Tammany politicians, evidently selected for the purpose, and which assembled shortly after the election, with the cry of frauds on the elective franchise ringing in their ears upon every side, could find nothing in that direction worthy of injuiry, but devoted their time to a Paul Pry endeavor to ascertain what, if any amounts of money Republicans had contributed towards the expenses of the canvass. And when, as has been testified to by a gentleman summoned before them, the direct offer to furnish proof of frauds in the election was made them by him, one of the jurymen "replied that I (he) was not called for that purpose: that if they needed me (him) they would let me (him) know." The advantages and privileges enjoyed by, and the protection afforded to the adherents of Tammany, who for the benefit of the Democratic party engage in any form of illegal work which depraved ingenuity can devise, or wicked and abandoned characters perpetrate, could not be more forcibly shown. But one remedy remains—legislation. Congress can and must enact such laws as will prevent the recurrence of extensive frauds in repeating canvassing, etc., at future elections for President and Members of Congress. The present naturalization laws, embraced as they are in a number of statutes, should be repealed, and a general act, with every section carefully considered and explicitly expressed, should be passed. But nowhere is this more fully appreciated than at Washington. The only troublesome question has been as to what courts and officers shall exercise the power of making citizens. Probably not less than twenty bills on the subject of naturalization were introduced in the two houses at the last Session of the Fortieth Congress. That the matter was not acted upon at that time was solely because it was thought the wisest and safest course to await the report of the Committee investigating the frauds in New York. When that was received, as stated in the preface, no time remained. There will be, however, no unnecessary delay at the coming session, and one of the plans below mentioned will certainly be adopted.

I. The power to naturalize will be confined to the Circuit Court and District Courts of the United States, and the highest court of record in each State, or

II. Such power will be conferred only upon the United States Courts, Commissioners in Bankruptcy, and where necessary officers to be appointed by the President, or Chief Justice of the Supreme Court of the United States, to hold office during life or good behavior, and be known as Commissioners of Naturalization.

In either case the illegal action of judges, officers and clerks will be more closely guarded against than heretofore, and all derelictions of duty will be made punishable in the United States Courts. In the opinion of the writer the second method would be preferable, and the only objection which has ever, so far as his information extends, been made thereto, viz.: that it creates new officers, should weigh but little against the advantages and results derivable from its adoption. It is known to more nearly meet the views of the members of Congress from the Eastern and Middle States than any other. As originally proposed the measure restricted the right to naturalize to the United States Courts and the Commissioners in Bankruptcy. In this shape the Southern and Western members were strongly opposed thereto, such courts and officers being less numerous in their section of country than with us. The addition of the section providing for the appointment of Commissioners of Naturalization, who should hold court for the purpose of naturalizing in each county in their districts in each month, obviated this otherwise serious objection.

Among other measures tending to prevent and punish frauds upon the elective franchise which will be strongly urged, are bills drawn by the Hon. Wm. Lawrence, of Ohio, Chairman of the Committee which investigated the New York frauds, providing methods of punishing repeating, false registering, illegal voting, and fraudulent canvassing at elections for President and Members of Congress ; requiring Congressional Elections to be held on the same day throughout the Union ; and providing measures whereby a Presidential election may be contested. Thus much we are promised from the National legislature.

Let us now consider what, if anything, has been done or remains to be done by the State of New York. The last Legislature passed and the Governor signed a bill affixing penalties for any attempt to register or vote upon naturalization certificates known to be illegally issued or fraudulently procured. Beyond this the State could not go so far as preventing the future use of such certificates is concerned.

A bill to provide and punish frauds in canvassing was unfortunately not passed. The fact may be partially attributed to the resignation of the Hon. J. C. Bancroft Davis—now Assistant Secretary of State at Washington—who had the bill in charge. This bill should receive early attention from the next Legislature.

But the most important measure remains to be considered. Early in April, 1869, the attorneys who had represented the Election Committees of the Union League Club of New York in the Congressional investigation, and whose attention had been specially directed to every detail of the frauds, reported that if a few simple yet important amendments were made to the existing registry laws the opportunities for illegal conduct and action would be greatly lessened.

They were instructed at once to prepare and submit a bill embodying the proposed changes, to have it speedily presented in both branches of the State Legislature, and to urge its passage.

Acting under such orders a bill was drawn, and on the 10th of April introduced in the Senate by the Hon. A. W. Palmer, and on the 16th of the same month offered in the Assembly by the Hon. N. B. La Bau.

By hard work this bill was got through the latter body on the 4th of May, and passed the Senate two days later, and within a few hours of the final adjournment of the Legislature. Every Democrat in both houses strenuously opposed it for no apparent reason, save that it was what it purported to be, a bill " to ascertain by proper proofs the citizens who shall be entitled to the right of suffrage." By the State Constitution, all bills which having passed the Legislature shall not be returned by the Governor within ten days after presentation, become laws without his signature, unless the Legislature by adjourning shall have prevented such return: in such case they are dead. As the Legislature adjourned so soon after the passage of the act under discussion, it was feared by the advocates of the measure that the Governor, who it was never supposed would sign the bill, would carefully refrain from making public his objections thereto.

Most happily were they disappointed. On the 16th of May, Governor Hoffman sent the bill to the office of the Secretary of State without his signature, and with a singular lack of political sagacity accompanied the same with the following statement of his reasons for disapproving the measure.

In my annual message I took the ground that "there should be one Registry law for the whole State, imposing equal conditions and restrictions everywhere, and it should be the aim thereof to secure to every citizen his right of suffrage free from intimidation, corruption, or onerous exactions."

This bill not only makes regulations for the cities of New York and Brooklyn, differing from those which it applies to the other parts of the State, but it contains provisions likely to deprive honest voters of their rights, and to impede the free exercise of the suffrage.

Section 3 of the original Registry law, as amended by chapter 812 of the laws of 1866, provides that the meeting of the inspectors for final revision of the registry lists shall be held on Friday preceding the election, and that they shall, "on that day add to said lists the name of any voter who would on the first Tuesday of November be entitled to vote."

Section 3 of this bill abolishes the Friday meeting, and substitutes another day as the day of final revision, and does not re-enact, as applicable to the substituted day, or any other, this provision for adding the names of those who, not then entitled to vote, would nevertheless be so entitled on the day of election, by having meantime come of age. The law as it would stand, if this bill were approved, would exclude this class of persons from a constitutional right

Section 4 of the bill provides that if one inspector choose not to declare a man's name to be on the list, his voice shall not be received, or, if received by the Board of Inspectors, such vote shall not be counted in any subsequent "legislative or judicial scrutiny" of the election. The bill provides only that a special list be kept of the persons whose votes shall be received under such circumstances, but it is obvious that to make the the provision that the vote shall not be afterward counted effectual, not only the voter but his ballot must be identified.

This could only be done by marking the ballot, and although the law does not authorize this to be done, yet the practice of doing so would be apt to grow up. To do this would violate the secrecy of the ballot. As the existing election law requires that all ballots for any officer by whomsoever cast, shall be deposited in the one box provided for such ballots, it is plain there is no other way of carrying the provision into effect, except by marking the ballot or compelling the voter, in the subsequent scrutiny to reveal how he voted. Both these methods would be in violation of every elector's right to vote by secret ballot.   JOHN T. HOFFMAN.

With the Governor's objections before us, let us examine the provisions of the bill and review the statements of the veto.

In considering the bill we shall note the changes which it would have made in the existing laws and the occasion therefor. The first section simply substituted Tuesday four weeks for Tuesday three weeks before the day of election as the time for the first meeting of the Boards of Registry. The second section provided a new method of registering which, while simple and easy of execution, could but prove of incalculable benefit in the prevention of fraud. Under the existing law the inspectors register the names of the voters alphabetically, according to their respective surnames, so as to show in one column the names in full, and in another column the residences. By the plan proposed, the names of the voters in each house would be registered under the number of the house and street in which they reside.

As now conducted, it is evident that it is beyond the power of the inspector, without a long and tedious search through every letter of the alphabet and on every page of his register, to ascertain who or what number of persons have registered from any given house. Yet this is information he should be able to obtain at a glance. The election districts in New York city seldom, if ever, exceed three or four blocks in extent—some are but two—and there is rarely a district of which at least one of the inspectors is not a resident, or personally acquainted with most of the legal voters; nevertheless, the fact is notorious that from the very necessities of the case and the occasion, men are often times illegally registered, frequently a large number, from the residences of persons well known to the inspectors, whose attention is first drawn to the fact after the close of registration, when the evil is done and the remedy substantially gone. If, however, the mode suggested had been adopted, the moment an address was given, as the inspectors turned to place on the registry the electors name, the house by street and number would he brought prominently to the attention of at least some one of the Board, who would remember its precise locality, who owned, who resided there, and whether it was a private residence, boarding house, hotel or tenement. In short, an opportunity for the detection of fraud would be presented, which under the present law does not exist.

The third section provided that registration should close on the second Monday preceding the day of the general election. This would allow six working days to intervene, whereas under the existing law there is but one. The justice and propriety of this change must be evident to all when it is remembered that in most of the cities of our State, especially in New York where were registered last fall over one hundred and seventy thousand names, nearly one-half of the entire registry is made up on the last day or days, while under the existing law no opportunity is afforded for scrutinizing and verifying the lists, canvassing the several districts, preparing challenge books, and otherwise endeavoring to secure a fair and honest expression of the public will, prevent the polling of illegal votes, and provide for the arrest of those who would violate the laws and usurp or destroy the rights and liberties of the people. Bad and designing men have simply to refrain from registering until late in the afternoon or evening of the Saturday preceding the day of election (Tuesday) when within sixty hours thereafter—forty of which are either sacred to religion or devoted to rest—they are able to vote without fear of detection, and against the will of the lawful electors to place in positions of honor, trust and profit, executive, legislative and judicial officers.

The more important features of the fourth section provided that two inspectors of different political faith, should each have sole charge of the registry on the day of election, for the purpose of checking the names of those who voted, and that a uniform mark should be used as such check. Also prohibited the receiving of any vote until the said two inspectors should have found and declared the elector's name to be on the register. The objects aimed at by these provisions were all attempted to be covered by section six of the act of 1865, but the more thorough detail of this bill and the addition of a clause requiring any violation thereof to be noted in writing in the inspectors' books, and making such violation a misdemeanor punishable by heavy fine or long imprisonment, or both, would, it was believed, secure a more perfect compliance with the law on the part of its officers. It is well known that a large number of votes have been received at every election without time being allowed the single inspector, who, under the present law, is placed in charge of the check copy of the register, to ascertain if the parties offering to vote were registered, while it is equally notorious that hundreds of votes were polled in the city of New York at the election last November—and this must have been with the aid and connivance of said check inspector—who were *never registered.*

By the change proposed no *one* inspector or clerk could connive at the commission of fraud so deliberate and destructive as this, and the honor of the State as well as the general welfare would seem to demand that the opportunity should not be afforded. It will be observed, that, by the system of checking proposed, the check registers would show not only the number registered but the number of votes polled and the names of the voters, thus uniting in one book a registry and poll list, and affording a means of detecting fraud on the part of poll clerks or canvassers. To illustrate; it was testified to before the Congressional Committee that at the November election in the third district of the Fourth Ward of New York, during the absence of one of the poll clerks, his associate copied fom the register list in the hands of an inspector eighty-five (85) names which he added to both of the poll lists without the knowledge of the other clerk. When the canvassers took possession this number of votes was dropped among the ballots as they were turned from the boxes upon the table and counted in the return made, yet under the existing law no means are provided for the detection of so skillful a fraud.

The fifth and last section provided for the inspection of all registers and poll lists without charge, by any elector. This is substantially the present law, the amendment being merely adding the poll lists not now open to examination.

Let us now examine the Governor's objections to this seemingly just and necessary bill. They may be briefly stated :

I. Because the bill made " regulations for the cities of New York and Brooklyn, differing from those which it applied to the other parts of the State."

II. Because it contained " provisions likely to deprive honest voters of their rights, and to impede the free exercise of the suffrage."

There is a reference by the Governor to a portion of his Annual Message, in which he advocated a registry law for the whole State, but it is evidently not spoken of as a reason for declining to sign this bill, so that the two heads given cover his objections. The first is a statement of fact. The second of opinion solely. The former is true; the latter, as we shall show, is without foundation. But while admitting the charge of differing regulations for the Cities of New York and Brooklyn —and such differences have always existed, and must necessarily continue to exist—we are at a loss to know which of such differences the Governor disapproved of, for he utterly fails to designate it. Possibly all were distasteful, and so his language would imply, yet it is difficult to say why he sh ould disapprove of an additional day being allowed residents of New York and Brooklyn in which to register, or object to the Boards of Registry in those cities being compelled to hold sessions an hour earlier and two hours later than in the other portions of the State. Nor does it seem possible that he could have objected to a single additional copy of the registry being made in the City of New York, for the purpose of being filed in the office of the Bureau of Elections, or the requirement that the mark which inspectors must make in their check registers opposite the name of every person voting, should in New York and Brooklyn be similar to a letter V.

Indeed, we are confident no one will for a moment pretend to believe that the Chief Magistrate of the State of New York refused to sign this bill in consequence of these differences- Yet every provision making regulations for the cities of New York and Brooklyn differing from those applicable to the remainder of the State which are not specially included by the Governor as falling under his second objection has been mentioned save one.

The exception consists in the requirement that in every district in New York and Brooklyn, two inspectors, one of each political faith, shall each have on the day of election the sole charge of a copy of the registry for the purpose of checking the names of such persons as vote. No change in this respect was made in the remaining districts of the State, the existing law directing one inspector to keep such copy, but not preventing two from so doing if they chose. It would hardly seem that this simple provision could have caused the Governor to withhold his signature, but doubtless it did, and a reason for such belief can be readily given. Prior to the year 1868, acting under the existing law, the Democratic Board of Supervisors of Kings County, who had the appointment of all election officers, had uniformly followed the practice of the Republican Board of Police Commissioners in New York, and divided such appointments equally between the two political parties. At the election in 1868, when Hoffman was the candidate of his party for Governor, the Democratic majority in this Board of Supervisors, acting if we may judge from its proceedings under a preconceived and fixed plan, held a quasi secret session, and appointed the election officers. Their selections being made known, it was found that with hardly an exception, every inspector of registry and elections was a Democrat. The same condition of affairs would have existed in New York had the Democracy had a majority of the Board of Police Commissioners. The section of the bill last noticed, in providing for the checking of the registry by two inspectors, and requiring each to be of different political faith, would have prevented the repetition in the future of any such proceeding, and always secured the minority one out of the four inspectors.

The honest and fair minded of all parties will not only believe the provision eminently wise and proper, but somewhat less than just. The Governor, grateful to his party for their conduct and course, could only regard it as an objection to the bill and a hindrance to future partisan action on behalf of himself and his political friends.

But we pass to the consideration of the second and last objection. The bill, says the Governor, "contains provisions likely to deprive honest voters of their right, and to impede the free exercise of the suffrage." Fortunately, these provisions are designated by the Governor, and his views thereof expressed at length, wherefore we may examine them both and see not only if the fact be so, but if his arguments are correct. He first says that by chapter 812 of the laws of 1866, the Friday preceeding the election was designated for the meeting of the inspectors to finally revise the registry lists, and that said inspectors were by that law required " on that day to add to said lists the name of any voter who would on the first Tuesday of November be entitled to vote." That the words are correctly quoted by the Governor no one will dispute. He adds that section 3 of the bill under discussion amends so much of chapter 812 as fixes the Friday before election for final revision by substituting the " Tuesday, one week preceding the day of the general election" as the time for such revision. This is true, and the Governor makes no objection to the change. Proceeding, he says this bill " does not re-enact as applicable to the substituted day, or any other, this provision for adding the names of those who not then entitled to vote, would, nevertheless, be so entitled on the day of election by having meantime come of age." Again correct. But adds the Governor: " the law as it would stand, if this bill were approved, would exclude this class of persons from a constitutional right." Here we beg leave to differ with our Chief Magistrate. Only so much of the law of 1866 would have been changed by this bill as was expressly amended. All that was not altered would have remained in force. Now, as this bill only changed " the Friday preceding the election," as the day of final revision, to the " Tuesday, one week before the election," the remainder of the section providing for the registration of the class referred to by the Governor would have remained as operative as before. It is painful to think that the Governor allowed his party zeal to so affect both his mind and his official action as to cause him to wholly overlook so apparent a fact. But again. The law of 1866 seems to have been worded with the very change proposed in this bill in view. After fixing a day for the revision of the registry, it reads: " And they (the inspectors) shall *then* revise the said lists and shall on *that day* add the names of those who would be legal voters on the day of election." Whether the words " then" and " that day" refer only to the day named, " Friday," or are to be considered more general and to mean *the day of revision*, may be somewhat questioned. The writer believes the latter is the true application. But grant that the Governor's assumption is correct, and the Friday before the election is the day indicated. Immediately following in the same section we read: " But in making such addition on that day, (Friday the Governor says, and for argument's sake we admit it,) *or any prior day*," the inspectors shall conform to the requirements of the other provisions of the registry laws prescribing their duties. If the interpretation of the Chief Magistrate is correct, we should be pleased to know what the words " or any prior day were inserted for."

Do they not clearly imply that another day prior to Friday preceeding the election, may be named for the revision of the list, and that " then," and " on " that day—the day of revision—the names of certain persons shall be added? We so think, and with the knowledge that the bill objected to by the Governor designated a " prior day" for such revision, and the well known rule of law and parliamentary usage that whatever of a law is not repealed by a subsequent act remains alive and of legal effect, it is exceedingly difficult to believe the class of persons spoken of by the Governor would or could be excluded " from a constitutional right."

The next provision, which the Governor thinks "likely to impede the free exercise of the suffrage " is contained in section four of this bill. He states it as follows: "That if one inspector choose not to declare a man's name to be on the list, his vote shall not be received, or if received by the Board of inspectors, such vote shall not be counted in any subsequent legislative or judicial scrutiny of the election." The Governor is here a little unfortunate in his language. What the section under discussion did require may be learned by referring back to the foot of page 25, where it is fully set forth. The existing law declares, "Nor shall the name of any person be placed or retained on such register without the concurrence of three of the four inspectors." It also provides that no vote shall be received save from a person found to be previously registered, wherefore it follows that no person can vote unless three of the inspectors consent thereto. As well might the Governor say that under that law "the free exercise of the suffrage " is impeded, because if two inspectors choose not to place a man's name on the list, his vote can not be received. Yet no difficulty was found in 1868 in registering 170,222 names, and polling 156,060 votes in New York city. The necessity for the objectionable provision has been fully shown, and it is only needed to direct attention to the heavy penalties attached to the refusal or neglect of any officer of election to properly discharge his duties, and which were never before a part of any registry act, for all to understand how trifling and untenable is the Governor's position. To that portion of the section requiring a list to be kept of all votes received contrary to the provisions of the bill, and forbidding that any such votes should be counted in any " legislative or judicial scrutiny," the Governor also objects, and quite naturally. For while the existing and all prior laws have contained in the very words of this bill the prohibitory portion of the clause, the requiring of a list of such illegal votes to be kept, would greatly aid a contestant who believed himself wrongfully kept from his rights, and prove beneficial in preventing fraudulent voting and connivance thereat on the part of election officers. The Governor attempts, at the close of "his objections," to argue for a secret ballot, apparently forgetful that by the State Constitution and the decision of the Court of Appeals, all voting is and must be by secret ballot. The pretense, that in order to throw out any illegal vote in the event of a " legislative or judicial scrutiny," it would be necessary (although the bill " does not authorize this to be done," the Governor says) to mark the ballot is so foolish, shallow and untrue, as to be unworthy of notice. With hardly an exception, not a legislative session, state or national, has been held for the last quarter of a century, without seats therein being contested, committees appointed, evidence taken, and the knowledge as to *how*, when and where an elector voted, obtained with comparatively little difficulty. But the Governor, having never served in a legislative body, and being still in the hands of his party trainers may have been ignorant of such fact, and innocently unaware of the rule of such bodies governing testimony and witnesses. We must, therefore, forbear all further discussion of the subject, for " where ignorance is bliss 'tis folly to be wise " was truthfully written long years ago.

"REDDY THE BLACKSMITH."

William Varley, *alias* "Reddy the Blacksmith," now an inmate of the Tombs, awaiting trial for the robbery of one Lawrence Graham, of New Jersey, who was enticed into his saloon in the cellar of No. 7 Chatham Square, is a villain of the deepest dye. He is 35 years of age, 5 feet 7 3-4 inches high—light complexion, with red hair and known to the police as a pickpocket, and a thief, large sandy moustache. Although very well he has always managed to escape punishment, for the reason that his valuable political services during the time of elections in manipulating votes and voters in the 4th and 7th Wards, could not be dispensed with by Tammany Whether he will be similarly fortunate this time is a question, the settlement of which is anxiously awaited by the public. The cut presented on a preceding page is from a picture for which "Reddy" sat a short time since.

Following the example of many illustrious predecessors "Reddy" rejoices in being the chief or leader of a gang or tribe which does him honor by bearing his name. It seems hardly necessary to add that "Reddy's" followers possess a name and character similar to their leader, although generally less widely known. The writer not long since came into possession of an authentic list of members of "The William Varley Association," and takes pleasure in being able to make their names public. They are:

William Varley *alias* "Reddy the Blacksmith,"
William Johnson,
Allen Martin, (?)
Charles Taylor,
William Manning,
Mathew Bannan,
James Moore,
Patrick Nolan, *alias* "John Reilly,"
James Walker,
John Finn,
Michael Cobey, *alias* Henry Williams, *alias* Charles Grant,
Richard Hayes,
William Brown,
Wall Walsh,
David Callahan,
Thomas Osborn,
William Burton,
Thomas Varley, brother of "Reddy,"
George Knowles,
Charles Wilson, *alias* Henry J. Lawrence, *alias* "Nibbs,"
Lawrence Fitzgerald,
Michael Varley, brother of "Reddy," *alias* Chas. Anderson.

The following is a literal copy of an original letter received by "Reddy" from a confederate incarcerated in the Tombs for theft, The original is now in the possession of the writer. As illustrative of the nature of the transactions of "Reddy" and his gang it is inserted.

December 28th.

friend Wm. Varley, will you Be so kind to send me Borack By some one if you cant come to see me yourself one Dollar and a bit of chuck for I am starving and perishing with cold. friend general it his not much I ask and you know if I get away you would have it—I geus you no that. Tom Davis was in here to see some one. I geus Dan Noble But passing my cell I called Tom and they stopt talking to me what I was in for and I told them and then ask me do go to down Reddys and I sayed yes. he then asked me how you was getting on and I told him you was Doing good and then Dan and him ask Did send me anything. I told I Did no Dout you would if you knew where I was. old general this fust I ever ask and I hope you wont Deny me it will not Break you nor make you. Give best wishes to your Wife Emma my Best friend. my respects to tom and Mickey.

tall Emma if I get away she would have the pleasure wearing one. she knows that.

I am in my own name Michael Sullivan, cell 99 third tier. old general you do that for me and it will be luck to you for you and Emma his the only tow friends i have. I geus sing sing this time. But never mind, ash for Breakfast and a shower Bath for supper. But they cant served me worst than I have Been. so no more at present from your well wisher. Borack for god sake Do it for I shall croak here with cold.

PATRICK H. KEENAN.

This gentleman is a Coroner of the City and County of New York. We have on page six referred to a gang of repeaters registering from his residence and given the portrait of the leader of the gang. Coroner Keenan being examined under oath by the Congressional Committee testified that but "three males" over 21 years of age resided in his house, himself, James Ryan and Denis O'Neil. The names of ten other persons, among which was that of Robert A. Jones, who had illegally registered therefrom, were then read to him and the question put him, if he knew men of those names. The reply was, "I do not." The officer who saw the registrations made testified that he knew Robert A. Jones, and that said Jones "goes (went) to Keenan's house a good deal, but he does (did) not live there." When the writer first noticed this discrepancy in the testimony he endeavored to believe that it was possible for Jones to visit Keenan's house considerably and Keenan not know him, as it might be that Jones visited Ryan or O'Neil, though the latter is Keenan's brother-in-law. Since then the author has received certain evidence which convinces him that the Coroner *did know* Robert A. Jones when he swore on the 31st of December, 1868, he did not. That each reader may judge for himself whether the fact is not so, the following paper, a copy of the original in the possession of the writer is appended.

New York, Oct. 27, 1868.

Sir:—A meeting of the P. H. Keenan Association will be held at No. 29 East Broadway, on Saturday evening, the 31st inst., at eight o'clock. Your punctual attendance is requested.

R. A. Jones, President.

E. N. Laffey, Secretary.

It should be remembered that 29 East Broadway, where this meeting of the Keenan Association was called for, was where Walling arrested the repeaters and seized their book. (See page six.) The evening, October 31st., was the night Judge Barnard discharged said repeaters. (See page seven,) and the hour for the meeting eight o'clock, was one hour after the time mentioned in the writ of *habeas corpus* procured by Counsellor Howe for the appearance of the repeaters at Judge Barnard's house. (See page eight.) A singular state of affairs certainly, but it must not be assumed that the arrested eight were anxious to attend the meeting of the P. H. Keenan Association. The writer has, however, an opinion upon the subject. Each reader will form his own.

JOSEPH FARRELL.

The portrait of this man as it appears in the Rogue's Gallery at Police Headquarters has been heretofore given. He is also known by the *aliases* of Lawrence Farrell and William Peirce. He is about 19 years of age, 5 feet 11 1-2 inches in height, of light complexion, and a burglar by occupation. Under the name of Lawrence Farrell he was brought before the Congressional Committee by one of the Democratic members. His direct examination was very brief, and elicited no

JOSEPH (ALIAS LAWRENCE) FARRELL, ALIAS WM. PIERCE.
Burglar, etc.. etc. (See Appendix.)

information, but upon being subjected to a severe cross-questioning he testified that he could furnish "a thousand persons" who had repeated at the Presidential election. His statement unsupported would be utterly worthless, but taken in connection with his admission that on the night before the election he was at the Jackson Club rooms, where Sheriff O'Brien was present, and a "lot of men" were congregated renders it probable that in this matter Farrell told the truth.

JAMES AND PATRICK GOFF.

These two brothers are the men referred to on another page as being engaged before the courts in obtaining fraudulent naturalization certificates. It was testified to before the Congressional Committee that an examination of the records on file in the Clerk's office of the Supreme and Superior Courts showed that these two individuals were accepted as witnesses to the residence and "good moral character" of *six hundred and sixty-six* (666) applicants. Of this number *five hundred and twenty-two* times and in the Superior *one hundred and forty-four*. Of the 27,068 certificates in the Supreme Court unaccounted for there is no method of ascertaining how many were obtained by these men. That it was a very large number there can be no doubt as it was sworn before the Committee that one of them was seen to have in his possession last Fall, in the opinion of the witness, "over *four thousand*" naturalization papers.

That the public may fully comprehend the character of the witnesses which satisfied Judges Barnard and McCunn as to the qualifications and "good moral character" of applicants for citizenship it is only necessary to add that the brothers Goff are well known disreputable and criminal characters. A member of the police force testified before the Committee that he had arrested both of them; that James was "*a professional thief*;" and that within forty-eight hours of the close of naturalization proceedings in the courts "James was arrested for stealing a gold watch and chain and two diamond rings." Of course they escape punishment.

JAMES O'BRIEN.

This individual is the Sheriff of the County of New York. He is about 29 years of age, some 5 feet 7 inches in height, of light complexion, smooth face and stout build. His early life was passed in the employ of a stonecutter. When about 18 he was a rested, indicted and convicted "of riot and assault and battery." Judge Barnard, then Recorder, sentenced him to "six months" imprisonment "in the Penitentiary of the City of New York," but he was pardoned by the Governor before the expiration of his term. He has since served as a member of the Common Council and for some two years past as Sheriff. We have heretofore referred to the characters of those who surrounded him and enjoy his confidence, and shall hereafter notice others of his more promising and trusted satellites. It was established before the Congressional Committee that on the night before the election there assembled at the rooms of the Jackson Club—an association of which the Sheriff is a prominent and active member—some two or three hundred men. That a large number of those men remained there all night, and before daybreak on the following morning were piloted to what they were informed and believed was the Sheriff's residence where breakfast was furnished them. Their hunger being satisfied they were shortly started out, and furnished from the Club House and elsewhere with names and residences upon which they voted throughout the day in the most reckless and extravagant manner. The Sheriff being examined as to these matters admitted his connection with the Jackson Club; that he was present at the Club rooms the night before election; that a large number of men were there at that time;

and that on election morning he kept "open house from five to six o'clock" and breakfasted a considerable number of men.

DAVID MYERS,

alias David Mullen, is a Till Tapper, about 25 years of age and 5 feet 6 1-2 inches high. The cut we have published is engraved from a photograph in the Rogue's Gallery. He was arrested on the 28th of November, 1868, together with two other disreputable characters, on suspicion of Grand larceny, but on examination before a magistrate was discharged. On the person of one of the men was found a warrant appointing David Mullen a special Deputy Sheriff to assist in preserving the public peace at the time of the election.

PATRICK McCAFFREY.

This man was formerly a special Deputy Sheriff. Quite naturally he was found largely engaged in procuring fraudulent naturalization certificates. It has been testified that his name appears as a witness two hundred and fifty-one times in the Supreme Court, and upon two hundred and fifty-two applications in the Superior. A total of *five hundred and two* persons known to him to be of "good moral character" and entitled to naturalization.

JOHN MORAN.

During the time when the Supreme and Superior Courts were engaged in naturalization this man was one of the most active and earnest participants in the work of obtaining fraudulent certificates. It was testified to before the Committee that in the Supreme Court he appeared by the records to have been a witness for *four hundred and fifty-five* (455) applicants, and in the Superior for *two hundred and ninety-nine* (299), or a total of *seven hundred and fifty four* (754) persons. Of these *one hundred and twelve* in a *single* day in the Supreme Court. A most excellent witness as to qualifications and "good moral character." For some reason shortly after the election he entered the employ of the Sheriff, and for conniving at the escape of a noted bond robber placed in his custody for delivery at the State Prison, was subsequently convicted and sentenced to imprisonment in Sing Sing, where he is supposed now to be.

FLORENCE SCANNEL

is a man of about 5 feet 6 in height, light complexion and stout build, with a chestnut and muscular development such as the writer never saw equalled. He is about 23 years of age, a butcher by trade, and the owner of one or more valuable stands in West Washington Market. His ostensible business is styled by him as "horse trading," though the police, who are thoroughly acquainted with the details, designate it by a name more in accord with its real nature. During the war Scannel was largely interested in faro banks in Washington and Alexandria, and, as we are informed and believe, now "runs a small game" in Fourth avenue, near Twenty-seventh street, which nets him a monthly income of some $1,600. His education is somewhat limited, but enables him to read print quite readily and write his name in a very fair hand, but it is with difficulty he can read the most ordinary words when written. He is exceedingly popular with the "b'hoys," and prides himself on a reputation of being a teetotaller. In politics Scannel is an unadulterated Democrat of unbounded pluck and rare political strength. He was chosen to a seat in the Board of Councilmen in 1866. As will be seen on page nine, Scannel was examined as a witness before the Congressional Committee. His appearance and manner were striking and peculiar.

At the close of the examination being informed that he might go he turned to the Committee and in his blandest tones said : "Well gentlemen, I bid you good day. I have no doubt we shall meet again, for I'm coming down there to Congress some day. You may just bet your lives I am." His belief and prediction were speedily verified, although not in the manner threatened, for having in response to a question of the Committee refused to answer, adding " I would rather go to the Tombs all my life than do it," he was arrested, brought before the bar of the House of Representatives and directed to answer the question. Still refusing, claiming that he had forgot ten the desired facts, he was fined the cost of his arrest (some $75) and incarcerated in default of payment. Preferring to enact the role of a martyr to paying the fine he was furnished quarters in the basement of the Capitol for some five weeks, and until the adjournment of Congress.

JOHN T. HOFFMAN.

On the 3 st of October, the day on which Inspector Walling arrested the repeaters and seized their books, and the day on which Judge Barnard illegally released those repeaters, the then Mayor of the city of New York, now Governor, and prospective Democratic candidate for the Presidency issued a proclamation. He charged I. that "gross and unfounded charges of fraud are being made * * against those high in authority." II. That "threats are made against naturalized citizens, and the authority of the judges and the seal of the Supreme Court is defied." III. "A grand jury of the United States Court summoned through the agency of those who are in this scheme has, as I have been informed, been induced without that preliminary examination which is usual, and which is afforded by law for the protection of character to find in great haste and secrecy bills of indictment against divers persons f r the purpose openly avowed of intimidating them in the discharge of their public duties." IV. "The United States Marshal * * has assumed to himself the power and duty of appointing swarms of special deputies to take their place at the polls to threaten and awe the electors of the State of New York in the exercise of their high privilege of casting their votes for the chief officers of the nation and the State." These several acts the Mayor proceeded to say were done "for two purposes."

"First. To conceal and cover their own schemes of fraud which they hope to consummate by the aid of untried or unpardoned criminals.

Second. So to excite the masses of people in this city who are opposed to them as to lead them into acts of disorder and violent resistance."

Mr. Hoffman was called before the Congressional Committee and being sworn was very severely examined upon each of these points. The writer never saw a more pitiable spectacle than the Mayor presented at that time. But our readers may judge thereof for themselves. Not a single charge contained in the proclamation could the Mayor sustain in any way. He swore that it "was common report based on the statements of many individuals," &c., that threats were made against naturalized citizens, but stated that he could not mention the names of a single person who made such a statement. He swore that "it was announced in many of the papers," &c., "that the registrars * * * had a right to go behind the certificates of naturalization * * * to deny the validity of them, to examine into their genuineness or irregularity, and to refuse to register, if in their judgment they thought proper so to do," but that he could not furnish a reference to any such newspaper. He swore that he "had no knowledge" of the issue of fraudulent naturalization papers, although "such charges were made in the papers," and that he took no steps to ascertain the correctness of such charges. In reference to the third charge of his proclamation he swore that it was so "generally under

stood in the city," although he could not give the name of "any person" who so stated, and he did not believe the United States grand jury "had been summoned or procured to be summoned in any other than the legal and usual way," or that the indictments found by it "were found without the examination that is usual by grand juries in that court." He swore in reference to his fourth charge that it was so "generally understood," but that he took no steps to ascertain from any official source whether it was true or not. Marshal Murray testified that he did not appoint a single deputy. In reference to the first purpose for which he charged these things were attempted, the Mayor swore that he had "merely the statements made to me (him) by confidential friends and the District Attorney in reference to Theodore Allen for whose arrest a bench warrant had been issued which the police "would not execute." There were others he believed mentioned by the District Attorney, but their names were not given him, and he took no steps to ascertain their number. He swore that he supposed he had evidence that republicans were engaged in schemes of fraud, because they held certain secret meetings, and for the reason that "it was very well understood that immense sums of money were being contributed by very wealthy men, candidates for office and others." This and this only was the purport of the Mayor's justification for his wicked and lying proclamation.

It speaks for itself in every particular, save the reference to Theodore Allen. Let us therefore ascertain the facts in that matter.

Mr. A. Oakey Hall, then District Attorney being examined as to the information given Mayor Hoffman by him in this matter, testified that he knew of but a single case. That it was not Theodore Allen but one Wesley Allen for whose arrest the bench warrant had issued. That said warrant "was out three weeks before the election, and was never executed until after the election, although the man was in the city, and I, (Dist. Attorney Hall) could have arrested him at any moment."

It would seem therefore that the "untried or pardoned criminals" charged by the Mayor as about to be used by the Republicans to conceal and cover their own schemes of fraud, consisted of one individual, Wesley Allen who was in no manner charged to be or ever to have been a Republican, Capt. Mills to whom the bench warrant was delivered, and who in the language of the District Attorney is "a high minded, incorruptible, splendid police captain" was next examined. He testified that late in October he received from the District Attorney a bench warrant for the arrest of Wesley Allen, with positive instructions to let no one know that he had such warrant. That acting under such orders he made every possible exertion to find Allen, even visiting Brooklyn "and other places where he frequented" for that purpose. That he communicated the fact of his having the warrant to no "living soul," not even to his own sergeants or the police superintendent, but that it was not until the 16th of November that he was able to find Wesley Allen, when he at once arrested him. Thus it will be seen that in every respect Capt. Mills performed his whole duty. It may not be uninteresting to our readers to add that Capt. Mills further stated, and this will show the force of Mayor Hoffman's charge as to pardoned criminals, "that Wesley Allen was a notorious thief," who had twice been to State's Prison, but that his second term had been shortened by a pardon granted by Governor Fenton, upon the application of District Attorney Hall and others. And that Mr. Hall had himself stated to him this was the fact, and that he (Hall) was "satisfied Allen was not" guilty of the crime for which he was sentenced—and still further—upon arresting Allen he was turned over to the District Attorney and incarcerated in the Tombs for about a month, "when he was set at liberty."